FALLING FOR CHRISTMAS

Ernest Michael Olivarez

Copyright ©2025 Earnest Michael Olivarez;
Falling For Christmas

ISBN: 978-1-7328080-4-1 (Paperback)
ISBN: 978-1-7328080-7-2 (ebook)
Library of Congress Number: 2025905095

Disclaimer: This book is a work of fiction. Any references to historical events, real people, or real places are used fictitiously. Other names, characters, places and events are products of the author's imagination, and any resemblance to actual events or places or persons, living or dead, is entirely coincidental.

Published by

Earnest Michael Olivarez Book Publishing LLC

TABLE OF CONTENTS

Prologue

A New Beginning

The beauty of life flips everything upside down in ways I never imagine.

My full name has four parts: Maria Victoria Consuela Cruz. Try squeezing that onto a name tag. I grew up in a luxurious world wrapped in silk and stitched together with golden threads. My childhood means penthouse views, ballet lessons in Paris, and birthday parties with guest lists more curated than a Met Gala. The only thing I ever lack is space to breathe. My parents draft a plan for my life in ink so permanent, it seeps into my skin.

Back then, my schedule includes Ivy League cocktail hours and relationships that look perfect in photos but feel like nothing at all. I'm not exactly known for warmth. Or depth. Or any sense of real connection.

I exist as a beautiful mannequin—Golden blond hair, hazel eyes, and perfectly posed, hollow inside.

Right after graduation, I do what every wealthy girl with an identity crisis does—I escape to Europe. I call it "finding myself," but mostly I stumble into overpriced wine and blurry selfies next to monuments I can't name. When I come home, I land a cushy position at my father's company. Title: something impressive. Effort: minimal. I coast. I float. I exist.

Until the day everything changes.

I'm on my way home from meeting yet another guy my mother claims is "a perfect match." Her track record? Flawlessly bad. This one's obsessed with video games. I'm obsessed with… nothing, really. But on that day, the universe cracks open. And through that tiny, unexpected crack, something surprising slips in.

A second chance.

Fittingly, it happens around Christmas. If you'd asked me back then, I'd tell you Christmas is my least favorite season. Fake smiles, hollow laughter, a frenzy of forced joy and commercial chaos. The whole thing feels like a glittering lie.

But now, I stand beneath a sky strung with lights. My breath curls in the icy air. My heart—once guarded and still—beats in a rhythm that feels new. Lighter. Braver. More alive.

So if you're willing, I'll tell you what happened. How a spoiled, drifting girl with an overstuffed name finally found something real.

And maybe—just maybe—how I fell for Christmas.

Chapter 1

Maria's Freefall

A storm reveals the airport's geometric roof while powdery snow swirls over the runway lights like confetti caught in strong winds. A shuddering breath escapes me as the cold makes me grip my phone tightly because its surface feels icy against my ear. During my conversation with Dad I inform him about completing the quarter's financial analysis but my voice breaks due to stress. I put my gloved hand against my chest while I wait for his confirmation after saying "The northern branch is bleeding red."

Before he speaks the line remains quiet with a humming tone. His voice returns—unyielding strength wrapped in warmth. "Mija, numbers aren't the whole story. You can't slash lives on a ledger. His words reach me as fleeting flashes of distant light when he says we'll sit together after I land. I force a laugh. "Te quiero, Papá. I'll sleep on it."

The wind takes my breath away while he softly says, "Te quiero, mija." Travel safe. You need to put on some weight so you don't come off as too thin." I laugh out loud, "¡Ay, Papá!"

The limo drives up to the VIP entrance and leaves a trail of exhaust sounds. I push open the door grab my carry-on bag and walk in with visions of sleeping beneath the New York skyline filling my thoughts. The memory of my mother's blind date fiasco haunts my thoughts like a high-school soap opera. I push a loose piece of hair back behind my ear while standing at the private-jet desk. "Company jet to New York, please."

The attendant's fingers tap the screen. He lifts his head and his breath forms misty clouds due to the chill. The attendant's words of regret hit me harder than the raging storm outside. "There must be something—" I begin.

Another staffer drifts closer. "Trains are running. The Winter Express train departs from the station next door.

A train? As the wind cuts through my coat I scrunch my nose. "Fine." I shove past the glass doors.

Inside the station, chaos reigns: Travelers and their children struggle with bags in the station which features fake pine decorations and flashing reindeer lights at every turn. The station reverberates with holiday carols bouncing off tiled floors while vendors promote cocoa from their carts. The cheer feels plastic—an annual masquerade. A stuffed reindeer toy blocks my way on the platform. On impulse, I kick it. The stuffed animal reindeer flies to the side of the walkway. A boy's sob echoes in my ears but I continue forward without turning around.

I step onto the train and make my way to the back caboose bar. The dark walnut paneling shines brightly from brass sconces while burgundy leather banquettes embrace every table. The host receives my coat while I settle into the plush velvet cushions. A bored waitress hovers. I request an extra-dry martini with a twist while staring intently at my phone screen.

She moves away with grace and comes back in a precise sterile manner. I sip—vermouth floods my tongue. I slam the glass down. "This is wrong. Where's the vermouth flush?" She bristles. He responds to her concern with a knowing lift of his eyebrow. She backs away while complaining about impolite patrons and my accent which captures hearts.

My phone buzzes: Mom. I complain over tinny carols. My companion dedicated most of his time to video game entertainment. "Mom, I cannot hear you." I end the call.

I stand and search for silence. By the rear door the worker's parka hangs and I immediately put it on while pulling up the fur-lined hood. I step onto the narrow balcony. The wind cuts through my cheeks while frost nips at my lashes. My breath steams as the train shifts. I lose my balance and as my fingers slide from the handrail it slips away from my grasp.

The initial impact knocks the wind out of me, and time slows: gravity yanks me backward into nothing. The wind wails in my ears while I tumble down the hill. The snowflakes slice my skin like sharp glass pieces. I finally land on a roadway at the bottom of the hill. Am I dead?

My body remains motionless for a minute. My breath manifests as a white smoke in the air. My head throbs; my ribs ache. My vision blurs but reveals a sky populated by detached stars. I raise my shaky hands to touch my cheek which feels moist and heated. Blood or tears? The phone rests a foot away as its cracked screen emits feeble light. I try to grab the phone but discover my fingertips have lost all sensation.

A whimper breaks the stillness. My eyes follow the road where lights appear to shimmer from afar. Closer, I spot a tiny bundle in the snow: A puppy shakes on a patch of grass while frost sticks to his coat. His soft whine cuts through the cold.

"Oh, sweetheart." I crawl forward, chest burning. His big brown eyes meet mine while his tail shakes in response. I cup him in my hands. He nuzzles my neck, seeking warmth. My chest fills with a peculiar warmth which is less intense than anger yet more powerful than apathy.

I secure him in my parka by fastening the buttons along his back. He finds comfort against my chest while his whiskers graze my chin. My body rises and each movement causes sharp pain to shoot through my legs. "It looks like it's you and me." I say as I make my way down the road, walking towards the distant glow of lights.

About 5 minutes later the illuminated headlights from a solitary truck grow larger as it moves closer. The approaching truck leaves a crunching trail of gravel beneath its tires as it comes to a stop. The window rolls down. The man displays a worried expression under his frost-covered hair. "You okay?"

Relief washes over me. "I need a ride." I pull the car door open and step in shakily as heat rushes to my freezing limbs.

He watches me, eyebrows drawn. "What are you doing out here? Who are you?"

I prepare to speak but find nothing but silence in the room. My thoughts leave me with nothing to hold onto while my heart beats furiously. I blink at the snow-smeared window. One question echoes in the hollow: I don't know who I am.

Chapter 2

El Casa

Aidan's (pov)

There's a low rumble from my truck as I drive onto the gravel driveway. The fields stretch to either side covered by a heavy snow mat while each snowflake transforms porch light into gentle opalescent light. My breath materializes before me and instantly the familiar home comfort surrounds me—the pine aroma from my parents' living room filling the air and the warmth behind their walls promising protection. Tonight, though, I'm bringing someone unexpected inside. I gulp down my nervousness before I turn to look at the passenger seat.

The oversized olive-green parka she wears produces a crinkling sound with each of her movements. Her hood covers her face except for the golden hair peeking from her temples and the desperate grip she has on the small puppy that she holds close to her chest with both arms locked and white knuckles. From the roadside discovery until now she remained silent but her eyes darted upwards at me revealing wide uncertainty.

"Almost home," I murmur. She gives me a single, tense nod.

I shut down the engine and begin carrying the groceries from the backseat. As I open her door my cheeks are cut open by the biting cold. With a momentary pause she mounts the snowy running board while gripping the puppy with more strength. The puppy's nose shivers as it senses the freezing air.

The second Mom sees me walk through the door with a girl, something shifts. It's like a switch flips. One moment she's in sweatpants scrolling through recipe videos, and the next, she's gliding across the floor like she's hosting a five-star dinner party. "Mijo, come inside. It's freezing outside. And who is this with you? She asks." As she pauses and examines our new guest. "Someone I rescued, on highway 21" I announce, voice strained. "She needed our help."

Mom immediately puts our new guest at ease. She places her hand tenderly on her arm. "You're safe here, mija. Welcome."

As we step through the entranceway together we are immediately surrounded by the warm aroma of simmering cinnamon and the fresh scent of pine from the large Christmas tree. The living room glows: Red-and-gold garlands frame the windows while a tall tree twinkles with colored lights above which stockings droop before a crackling fireplace. The coffee table displays mugs of cider from which steam ascends.

I hang my coat up in the hallway, Our guest pulls away her hood and damp strands of golden-blonde hair fall onto her shoulders. My own breathing halts during that silent pause. Despite her messy appearance and her high cheekbones with eyes that show uncertainty she remains breathtaking. The woman releases the puppy from her arms so it rolls to rest at her feet while its gentle whine keeps her rooted in place.

A joyous squeal shatters the hush. "Daddy! "Daddy! A puppy!" Nichole's little feet patter across the hardwood floor. The girl skids to a halt beside the unfamiliar person and bends down to examine the shivering dog. The dog sniffs Nichole's extended fingers before giving her a cautious lick. Her face lights up.

The woman softly states "He's cold" while her words carry the tender melody of Spanish speech. "But I think he'll be okay now."

Nichole scoops the puppy into her arms. "Can we keep him, Daddy?"

My eyes meet Mom's and I see the same astonishment and happiness reflected in her expression. I answer with "We'll see," even though Nichole's hopeful grin makes my heart hurt. I haven't seen her happiness like this in such a long time.

The woman moves toward the fireplace while her gaze follows the decorations as though she has never seen Christmas before. She grasps a tiny plush reindeer from the mantel and spins it between her fingers. Recognition flickers across her brow, then fades.

Mom's voice is low and worried. "What happened, mijo?"

I step forward. At dusk I discovered her walking beside the highway. She was involved in a crash. I then explain that she cannot recall her identity.

"My Dios," Mom murmurs, stepping closer. She retrieves a wool blanket from behind the couch to cover the unknown woman. "Poor niña."

"Tomorrow, my daughter Sarah will drive you to the hospital for an examination and might assist with determining your identity." I mention that my old room is available for temporary use at this time.

Mom nods, already shifting into caretaker mode. "Let's get you fed and warmed up."

I lead the woman along the corridor towards my youth bedroom. When I open the door it reveals shelves with tarnished trophies and walls covered with framed sports photos which include pictures of me wearing my varsity jersey with a big smile. A layer of dust covers my old acoustic guitar which stands abandoned in the corner.

I casually mention that nothing has changed since I left.

She moves inside with caution while her fingers lightly touch the framed photographs. She gently shifts her gaze as she examines my old photographs.

My sister Sarah enters with arms full of stacked neatly folded clothes consisting of sweaters, leggings, and thick socks. "Here. These should fit," she says.

She acknowledges the gift by simply nodding. "Thank you. I—I really need a shower."

Sarah responds with a warm smile, "That's understandable." "Towels and toiletries are in the bathroom."

I clear my throat. "I have to go now and get Nichole to bed. We will stop by tomorrow to see how you are doing?

At Home, I discover Nichole in the hallway as she gently rubs her eyes. In a quiet voice she asks me "Daddy… can I sleep with the puppy?"

Her slight body settles against me as I lift her into my arms. "Maybe," I promise.

As I bring my sleeping daughter into her bedroom I picture the strange woman with her golden locks and haunted gaze who holds the puppy as if it's her lifeline. I positioned Nichole on the bed before planting a kiss on her forehead and observed her hug the plush reindeer as her eyes closed.

"Daddy…" she murmurs. "I really like her."

I pause at the doorway, voice thick. "I know, sweetheart. Me too." She smiles half asleep. "She needs our help right now mija."

Nichole squeezes her toy. "I think she's special daddy." I smile and glance at our family photo on the nightstand of all of us posing with that dumb Jose the Reindeer plush toy. Four years since the accident. I dedicated those four years to constructing emotional barriers within my heart. Tonight, though, something shifted. As I turn off the light, I realize now, that I may be entering a new phase in life.

Chapter 3

The Doctor's Visit

Sarah's POV:

Before I open my eyes I detect the spicy cinnamon and chile-scented steam curling under my door. My heart races as I sit up suddenly remembering Mom's morning magic with eggs sizzling like suns and tortillas crisping on the comal. Sleep envelops me but I can still observe her slender arms dusted with flour skillfully flipping tortillas in perfect rhythm while promising safety in silence. The atmosphere today buzzes with energy while the house seems to lean forward to eavesdrop.

I pull on a soft hoodie and step into my sneakers before walking softly down the hallway. At the kitchen doorway Mom places sizzling chorizo and steaming tortillas on Dad's worn plates next to the stove. He requires full calorie intake for his twelve-hour workday on the assembly line during the holiday season. The chorizo crackles, and memories of sacred Christmas mornings flood me: We stood beside each other in restless anticipation as we awaited her feast.

"Buenos días, mija," she says while facing away as her voice matches the comforting warmth of freshly poured coffee. "Come help me set the table."

I pick up the dark mug that retains traces of last night's coffee grounds and breathe in the bittersweet scent. I arrange tarnished forks and nicked knives while listening to soft footsteps behind me.

In the doorway stands a stranger: Her pale, slender figure is almost hidden by Aidan's oversized hoodie while her damp blonde hair rests behind her delicate yet glowing face. She appears suspended between hopeful anticipation and uncertain doubt as though she has emerged from a dream.

I gesture to the table and kindly ask her to come in and take a seat. "Aidan should be back any minute."

She steps through the doorway cautiously before sitting down on a wooden chair while her gaze stays on the tempting stack of tortillas. Mom takes her nurturing role seriously as she presents her with a full plate. "¿Quisieras un poco de café, mija?"

Her accent spreads through the kitchen with the soothing quality of a soft melody. With a shaky voice she shares her uncertainty about coffee.

Mom beams and fills a tiny cup with coffee. As we sit quietly in a symphony of dishes clinking together, steam dances through the morning light. I rip off a portion of the tortilla and feel the soft warmth of its dough before scooping eggs and refried beans onto it. The stranger instinctively follows my movements with her fingers as if she has performed this gesture countless times before.

I pause mid-bite, arching an eyebrow. "You know your way around a tortilla."

She blinks, caught off guard, then shrugs. "Sí… it just feels normal."

Mom watches her with gentle approval. "Así se come, mija. Here, no food is wasted."

Relief spreads across the stranger's face while her shoulders relax and she enjoys another comforting and familiar mouthful of warm food.

Soft conversation unfurls around the rising sun: Spoons clattered against dishes while Mom hummed softly and the coffee pot sighed its morning song. When we finish the last tortilla I settle back and tell her that we'll need her name if she's staying with us. Do you have any preferences?"

Her eyes dart toward the front door as though she anticipates Aidan—or a memory of him—walking through it. Finally, she whispers, "I don't know. How about… Jane?"

"Jane Doe it is," I declare, smiling. "Welcome to the family."

She responds with a shy smile. "Mrs. Martinez, this breakfast—es increíble."

Mom deflects the compliment while she continues to scoop more eggs onto her plate. "Eat, mija. You need every bit of strength."

After we finish eating I take my coat from the hook next to the door. "Alright, Jane. First stop: the clinic. After checking the clinic we will need to visit the police station to determine if anyone reported you missing.

Jane's shoulders stiffen, but she nods. "Okay."

The clinic smells like disinfectant mixed with polyester drapes. The doctor tests her pulse then examines her bruises that have started to fade while tapping his pen on the brochure about memory loss. "Could be hours before she remembers. He hands me the brochure with gentle concern as he states it could take weeks.

The police station contains nothing but empty files as there is no Jane Doe entry and no missing-person report aligns with her description. Her dark eyes show fear as she hears the officer say "I'm sorry" with tight lips.

I place my hand on her arm while we stand outside. "You okay?"

She manages to produce a smile that fails to touch her eyes. The experience feels odd because she doesn't understand who she truly is.

"Don't worry—We'll find out," I assure her as I draw her into a brief embrace before we go to my cousin's phone store.

He welcomes us while looking amused at her broken phone screen. He assures her he can repair the device but mentions he needs to order a replacement part.

Her bottom lip trembles. "I don't have any money."

Waving her away I say "You don't need to worry about it." "Consider it a welcome gift."

The diner sign changes to "Open" as we head back into the town and I give her a smile. "You ever wait tables before?"

Her head arcs backward as her laugh emerges with both brightness and nervous energy. "I have no idea."

"Perfect," I say. "We could use the help. Let's see what you've got."

She steps forward with a tray in her grip while holding a shaky water pitcher. Mugs overflow with coffee foam while she drops orders as fast as hot potatoes. I suppress my laughter while she offers multiple apologies to each customer in the row. Still, she doesn't give up. When she made her final coffee delivery she held glasses in one hand and menus in the other while standing with squared shoulders and eyes filled with determination.

Jane runs her hand softly across the table's scarred surface when we lock up for the night as though she wanted to remove the weariness that the grain shows. The long shadows stretch from the overhead lights while her face reflects a gentle inquisitiveness.

She questions softly about Aidan with a voice that trembles as if it were a page caught in a breeze.

My arms fold as I rest against the counter while maintaining a subdued tone. "He's kind. But he carries a sorrow—a deep grief. Four years ago Aidan lost his wife, Emma at this exact location where he first met you.

Jane's eyes widen, the pieces clicking together. That explains his peculiar gaze when he stared at me.

The dim illumination reveals her cheeks flushed with surprise and a hint of hope. "He hasn't really looked at anyone since. I think he sees something special about you.

She clenches her lip while her gaze lowers to the patched wood under her touch. "I don't even know who I am."

Gently, I place my hand over hers. "Maybe that's the best place to start."

Chapter 4

A Stranger in Kindness

Jane's pov:

I fall onto the bed and the mattress emits a groaning sound beneath my weight. Each muscle in my body protests my fatigue—I feel like I've spent the day lifting sandbags with my arms while my calves burn from continuous uphill climbs—and I follow the lifelines on my hand with a fingertip as if they were someone else's. They're too soft, almost unrecognizable. Have I ever worked this hard before? My hands performing tasks like scrubbing tabletops on the floor and maneuvering carts at the café no longer feel like they belong to me.

My spine sends a sharp pain outward until it reaches each of my fingertips. This strange tiredness is one thing, but the oddest part is the gentle warmth all around me: I hear muted exchanges from the hallway alongside the scent of cinnamon with fresh bread adhering to my clothes, while the Martinez family embraces me as if I'm family. They've provided me with meals, a place to stay… It's been nothing short of amazing. But, my personal experience has shown me that favors in business and daily life always attach invisible expectations. I still don't understand why they've accepted me without any conditions. What unspoken contract am I missing?

A gentle knock brings me back from my spiraling thoughts. I must've nodded off. The door emits a squeaky noise as Aidan enters the dimly lit hallway and softly calls out my name.

"Hey," I murmur, blinking. An amber light from the bedside lamp illuminates our feet. "Everything okay?"

He steps fully into the room. Mom and Dad are preparing a game in the living room. Thought you might want to join."

"A game?" My throat feels tight.

He leans against the doorframe, arms folded. "Yeah—just family time."

Family time. The words sound dense and unfamiliar but I manage to nod in response. "Okay."

We descend the carpeted stairs with each step groaning beneath us until we arrive in the living room. The stone hearth turns deep amber as firelight dances across it. The mantel displays draped pine garlands while the smell of orange and spice reaches me. A chunky board game occupies the center of the low wooden table while bright dice crowd around it together with plastic pawns of various colors.

Nichole sits cross-legged on the rug with her hair in two disheveled braids as she giggles while arranging her game pieces. Her eyes meet mine as the camera swings against her neck to take a picture. "Jane! You have to be on my team."

Aidan sits on the arm of his mother's favorite chair while wearing a teasing smile. "I don't know—she might beat you."

I raise an eyebrow. "Is that a challenge?"

His laughter radiates warmth which makes me forget my outsider status. The burgundy velvet armchairs become the parents' seat of refuge as they settle down. I sit on the sofa edge while its fabric presses against me and grab the dice with my trembling fingers.

I release the dice which scatter bright-red pieces across the game board. The sound of Nichole's triumphant whoop fills the room when my pawn lands on her square and I react with laughter. She snaps the picture—flash!—and holds it up. "Smile!"

I force my lips into a grin. She studies the photo and beams. The photograph captures Jose the Reindeer which invokes a distant yet comforting warmth inside me that I can't quite remember.

Aidan extends his body back while placing his feet on the coffee table. Aidan brings Nichole to this place during the holiday season. While my parents create Christmas enchantment throughout our house Aidan's silent moment as he examines the wood grain with his toe communicates volumes. Finally he murmurs, "It's... less lonely here."

Everything falls hush. The fire in the fireplace shifts to a continuous gentle light. Nichole pulls Jose close and gazes into his eyes while Aidan continues his conversation.

During one visit to my home he shared his experience about hanging some lights in his living room and purchasing a small tree before he sighed and shook his head. "It just didn't feel right. So we come here instead."

The sorrow he carries creates a painful twist in my heart which I had nearly forgotten amongst the sounds of dice and laughter. In the window's frost-flecked glass, I glimpse my own reflection: Though an outsider I remain and extend my reach toward things beyond my claims.

I prepare to speak by clearing my throat but the sound of my voice comes out sour.

Nichole moves nearer to Aidan and softly tells him that this year will transform because Jane has arrived.

Our gazes lock across the table and my body trembles. A strange combination of hopefulness mixed with fear and thankfulness causes my chest to tighten. While I can't say I'm prepared to sort through these feelings I remain determined to face all of them head-on.

Chapter 5

The Winter Festival

Aidan's pov:

Jane's been at my parents' house for almost a week now. I have to admit, it's been incredible having an excuse to come by more often—and to see her, too. For years I've just been... existing, going through the motions, shut down. But now, for the first time in a long time, I feel awake again.

It's Friday night, and dinner at my parents' is always an event. Tonight, though, Mom's really outdone herself. Her homemade sauce smothers the enchiladas, the cheese bubbles just right, and I can't stop shoveling forkfuls into my mouth. Jane and my sister Sarah tease me about my enthusiasm, but I don't care—I'll never tire of Mom's cooking. Even little Nichole is here, stuffing her cheeks, looking happier than I've seen her in ages.

Between bites, I glance at Jane. She eats so delicately, yet there's something eerily familiar in the way she folds her tortilla and scoops up beans—like she's done it a thousand times. Effortless. Second nature. A tiny window into a past she doesn't remember.

"Jane," I say, swallowing the last of my enchilada, "tonight kicks off our winter festival. Want to check it out with us?"

She hesitates a beat and then breaks into a radiant smile. "I'd love to!"

Sarah beams. "I know it's right after Thanksgiving, but this town lives for Christmas. We've got a card factory downtown, and you have to try Old Town Bakery's cookies!"

After dinner, Jane surprises everyone by gathering plates and stepping up at the sink without being asked. At first, her hands move a little uncertainly, as though washing dishes is brand-new to her, but she settles in and gets it done. Watching her, I feel this surge of something warm—like she really belongs here, even if I know she doesn't.

When we arrive at the festival, it's already in full swing. Pop-up shops line the streets, chestnuts roast on carts, and cinnamon drifts through the air. Ice sculptors chisel reindeer, angels, and towering Christmas trees, and string lights drape every building in a soft glow. And everywhere you look is Jose the Reindeer—plushies, ornaments, even a massive ice statue of him in the square. Nichole bolts ahead, snapping pictures with her little disposable camera.

I catch Sarah's eye and nod toward Nichole. "Take her for a snack, will you?"

She grins. "Oh, sure—go have your romantic moment."

I roll my eyes but turn to Jane and lead her across the square to the skating rink. Soft Christmas classics play from hidden speakers, the kind of music that makes you want to slow down and drink in every second. To my surprise, Jane is a phenomenal skater—far better than I am. She glides and twirls, her laughter light and free. It's the first time I see her truly letting go, unburdened.

"You've done this before," I say as she completes a graceful spin and skates back to me.

She looks momentarily startled. "I think I have."

There's something so vulnerable in her voice, like she's on the verge of remembering but can't quite get there. It stirs something deep inside me—an ache I thought I'd buried long ago.

A slow, romantic song drifts in, and suddenly the rink and the lights and everyone around us fade away. It's just her and me. My heart thumps. Do I lean in? Do I kiss her?

"Daddy! Churros!" Nichole's voice slices through the moment as she skates up, clutching a steaming churro, grinning from ear to ear. Jane laughs, stepping back from me as the spell breaks. I chuckle, rub the back of my neck, and take the churro from Nichole's sticky fingers.

A week slips by, and still no word from the police or my cousin about Jane's phone. If I'm honest, I don't mind. Having her here feels… right. And that terrifies me more than anything else. I barely let myself think what it might mean.

I catch myself watching her more often than I should—the way she scrunches her nose when she's concentrating, how she tucks her hair behind her ear without noticing, the gentle patience she shows Nichole. It's dangerous, how I feel around her.

"Want to go toboggan sledding with us on Sunday?" I ask one evening, trying to sound casual.

Her eyes light up. "Absolutely!"

I let out a relieved breath. I still haven't mustered the courage to ask her on a proper date, but thankfully my family seems dead set on doing that work for me. I've come a long way since the accident that changed everything… and I'm finally starting to hope again.

Chapter 6
Shadows of Loss

Aidan's pov:

It wasn't always like this.

Joy flowed into our home just like sunlight filters through lace curtains before everything fell apart. The sound of my daughter's radiant giggles provided our mornings with their musical backdrop during those days. During lazy afternoons we entered my parents' farmhouse where its red-tiled roof radiated in the summer sunshine. The kitchen emitted warm bread aromas while the garden outside the back door displayed vibrant orange marigolds and lavender blooms that danced in the breeze beside rose bushes heavy with luxurious petals. Our playful hide-and-seek game among the flowers occurred with my little girl's hand resting in mine while the garden seemingly whispered our laughter on the breeze. During that time life offered unlimited opportunities and dreams yet unnamed.

The morning unfolded exactly as every other one had before. Golden sunlight streamed through the porch slats creating alternating bands of light and shadow on the floorboards. I sat in my beloved wicker chair enjoying dark steaming coffee as Nichole expressed her imagination through colorful drawings. Delighted giggles from her combined with honeysuckle scents traveled across the porch on the warm breeze. I bent over to brush her stray hair behind her ear and said softly, "You will realize how much you are loved someday."

A solitary, forceful knock on the door obliterated the serenity with a thunderous impact. My chest tightened before I even stood. As I turned around a police officer wearing a perfect uniform entered the room with eyes that radiated both urgency and sorrow. With a voice quivering he announced, "Sir, there's been an accident. Your wife is trapped in her car."

The words struck me with the force of a physical impact. My hand received a violent shock when my coffee cup burst open releasing scalding liquid across the porch. The ground gave way beneath me and I shot up to my feet before toppling down the stairs. My heart pounded like a war drum as I dashed down the street and gasped for each breath while each second dragged on endlessly.

Chaos erupted at the curb. The ground was covered with glass shards resembling black diamonds beneath the flashing red and blue lights. Paramedics rushed to the scene where a mangled sedan lay with its front end warped into a horrific shape. The air stung with gasoline's metallic bite. Amid the twisted metal wreckage my wife was trapped with a dark halo of hair over her white porcelain face pinned beneath the steel. I knelt beside her disregarding shouted commands to hold her cold thin hand. With my voice breaking I whispered "It'll be okay...please don't leave us" and her eyelids opened for a second revealing eyes full of both love and fear that nearly shattered my heart. "I love you," she breathed. "Promise...you'll take care of Nichole."

The paramedics released her from her entrapment and placed her on a stretcher. While on my knees I screamed her name into the unresponsive sky.

During the following days everything became timeless. Our home remained quiet with remnants of former joy echoing through its vacant spaces. The vibrant colors of Nichole's forgotten toys mocked me while they lay abandoned in an unnoticed corner. Each night sleep shattered into pieces while the rain's drip against the window remained my sole unchanging sound. Inside me developed a dangerous combination of rage and hopelessness. Whiskey glasses became my hiding place from my pain although their bitter warmth could never stand in for her embrace. The bars engulfed me while I pressed myself against the rail and memories of her smile haunted me. Their car's backseat became the scene for countless nights when my parents discovered me crying and comforted me until I sobbed myself to sleep.

The stormy night forced me to stand on the porch while strong winds ripped my coat apart and rain poured down my face. I cried out at the railing, demanding answers from the void, "Why did you take her?" The thunder responded with an indifferent rumble. The immediacy of that moment engulfed me with an overwhelming sense of emptiness. A transition from violent storm to leafy whispers awakened within me thoughts of her tender smile and her conviction that love could defeat the darkest sadness just as dawn breaks the night.

I gradually came to understand that I could not give up. I remembered her plea: care for Nichole, keep loving. I made a commitment to stop drinking and work towards creating the life we had imagined together. The journey was hard to walk because I can still hear tire screeches playing in my head alongside a physical ache in my chest and trembling hands when I recall that crash. The steadfast support from my parents alongside my daughter's joyful laughter became the foundation as I began to rebuild my life. I found hope in small victories: I found peace after finally sleeping through the night without interruption.

I confront new opportunities today while wearing that tragic day as an open wound which stands as proof of my endurance and what I lost. The pain from my injuries persists but does not dictate my identity. With every sunrise, I choose to honor her memory: I honor her memory through fierce love while depending on my family and seeking light beyond the darkness.

Chapter 7

Sledding

Jane's pov (Maria):

Excitement pulses through my chest as we load into the trucks heading towards our favorite sledding spot in town. The reason for my anticipation of today remains unclear but I think it might be because I get to spend time with Aidan or because this place already feels like home with his family.

We sprint up to the hilltop where the cool air refreshes us. Nichole and I climb onto a sled as Aidan and Sarah go for another sled. As we hurtle down the hill we both laugh while the wind buffets our faces against the snowy backdrop.

Grandma and Grandpa show up and go for old car inner tubes instead of sleds. Before long, a full-blown snowball fight erupts. Aidan feels the full force of Nichole's snowball in his chest while I become trapped within the ensuing chaos. I haven't laughed this hard in ages.

My memory is blank of my history but I currently experience safety. I feel warm. And that's enough.

Our day of tobogganing from the giant tower ends when we head back to the snack pavilion. The outdoor heaters generate perfect warmth while we enjoy hot chocolate and cookies. Grandma brought tacos to eat which remain tasty even when they are cold.

Nichole tugs on my hand. "One more toboggan run?"

Sarah and I exchange a grin. "Let's do it," I say.

I show Aidan my biggest smile and take Nichole's hand so we dash toward the tower. He smiles while he puts another cookie into his mouth as we move forward.

After a long day we come back to the house while feeling tired and content. The moment we step inside, Nichole gasps. The floor is covered in shreds of Nichole's beloved Jose the Reindeer plush while the puppy stands guiltily in the corner with ears flattened.

Nichole cries out in despair as she begins to collect the shredded fragments. "I can't believe you destroyed it! Bad dog!"

I kneel beside her while tears start to form in my eyes and then I hug her tightly. "It's okay, sweetheart. I need Grandma's support so I turn to her and ask for confirmation. "Right?"

She nods. "Sí, mija. We will fix him."

Nichole sniffles. The toy was the last gift that Mommy ever gave me.

Her words settle heavily on my heart. I feel a pang of sorrow as I watch Aidan kneel beside her to pull her close and her attachment to him.

Mrs. Martinez expertly repairs Jose with her sewing skills. She unexpectedly demonstrates to Sarah and me how to sew. At first I struggle with the needle until slowly I learn how to use it. We successfully purchase a new plush toy and meticulously take parts from it to reconstruct our original Jose. Nichole's reaction upon seeing her restored reindeer will be priceless.

My eyes land on Aidan as we both lock sights. An unspoken but deeply understood change occurs between us. I finally experience a sense of belonging.

Chapter 8

Reflections of Love and Loss

Emma's pov:

Aidan's Perspective

The back porch becomes my afternoon refuge as I watch Jane meticulously repair the ripped seams of Jose the Reindeer. The unwavering attention Jane puts into her work while caring for Nichole produces a mixture of sweet and sorrowful emotions within me. Each careful stitch brings back memories of Emma—the woman who once became the center of my universe while she nervously introduced herself to my family for the first time.

My memories of that day remain strikingly clear. Emma reached our front door while her hands trembled and her eyes showed simultaneous fear and hope. The moment Emma burst into a deep genuine laugh my mother's skeptical gaze melted away as though every barrier dissolved. Her sincerity broke through my father's usual stoicism and brought a smile to his face. The moment Emma entered the space she radiated warmth which made me feel secure about our shared future.

Memories of Nichole's birth day emerge within my mind. The hospital room came to life with soft beeping sounds mixed with quiet prayers. Emma looked at our newborn daughter while tears sparkled in her eyes as I held her hand. Aidan she leaned forward and whispered softly that our love serves as our strength. Emma's promise to hold fast to hope continues to reverberate in my heart, blending with the fresh hope I see through Jane's compassionate care.

Despite losing so much I find hope in Jane's gentle touch because I feel God is leading me towards a new beginning. Our shared laughter along with built memories and love's promise show me that damaged hearts can resume their rhythm. I maintain that hope while leaning back, committed to respecting the past and accepting future possibilities.

Emma's Perspective

The edge of memory holds me where I first entered Aidan's world. My family meeting felt like a test when my hands shook and my voice quivered from the fear of their evaluation. My words tangled as I struggled to show how much my heart was invested. Slowly, though, their hearts opened to me. My future mother-in-law's cautious smile transformed into warmth while his father who usually kept his feelings close showed his approval of my sincere dedication.

Those early days remain etched in my memory through the laughter that filled them. My casual joke built a connection between us while confirming my place in their family. I didn't rely on grand gestures but on small, heartfelt moments: The quiet grace of a timid smile blended with the comfort of a gentle word and the intimacy of a shared secret. Every small connection I made brought me nearer to becoming part of the family I wanted to join.

The moment when Nichole entered the world remains deeply imprinted on my soul. Between the constant monitor beeps and my rapid heartbeats I took Aidan's hand in the packed hospital room while I softly spoke vows of strength. I promised to be his steadfast support through every difficult time. Although our shared future ended abruptly and harshly I remain confident in the power and authenticity of our love.

The beauty of my past choices reveals itself to me as I dwell on these memories. My heart carries hope and sorrow but tells me that light survives all loss. The love I gave together with the promises I made create an enduring echo in Aidan's soul that pushes him forward even as darkness surrounds him.

Aidan's Perspective

As I sit on the porch I sense Emma's gentle spirit blending together with Jane's new beginnings. I choose to trust in God's guidance as I rebuild my life between what I've lost and what I'm starting to create anew. My heart holds its scars but pulses with renewed hope knowing that my future will overflow with love and warmth and the lasting memories of those who influenced me.

Chapter 9

Shadows of the Past

Jane's pov:

I emerge from sleep with a pounding heart and cold sweat covering my skin. A dream fragment persists in my mind where I stand in a harshly lit boardroom while angry faces surround me and my voice slices through the tense atmosphere. "Did I really do that? Did I really become that person?" I whisper into the darkness while my breath shakes. The specific moments fade away yet the cold ambition that trampled over everyone remains a stark reality. A shiver races down my spine. Should those memory fragments hold truth then I must question my identity.

My hands cradle my face as guilt and fear twist inside my chest. Aidan and his family have shown me so much warmth and kindness which is unimaginably different from the cold and calculating person I remember. "I don't deserve them," I murmur.

The light of morning filters through the curtains yet delivers no solace. I put on my clothes automatically and smile politely at the breakfast table as I breathe in the scent of coffee and pancakes without experiencing any taste. Working through orders and dishes at the diner distracts me while the clatter of plates sounds empty to my ears. Then I look up and freeze. I notice Aidan sharing laughter with a young woman through the bakery window from across the street.

My tray escapes my grasp and smashes against the floor. The world stops for a heartbeat before it springs back to life. Tears sting my eyes as I rush into the kitchen. Sarah follows, concern etched on her face. "Jane, what's wrong?"

Through broken breaths I tell her "Aidan is in a relationship with someone else."

Her eyes soften. "That's Liz—his late wife's younger sister. Nichole gets visits from her here.

Embarrassment burns me. "I... I didn't know."

Sarah squeezes my shoulder. "It's okay. But you should talk to him. Both of you require an opportunity to communicate and understand one another.

Her words give me courage. I inhale quickly with shaky breaths before entering the bakery. A welcoming chime sounds as the smell of freshly baked bread and sugar envelops me like a warm embrace. The wooden tables are draped with fairy lights as warm light cascades across them. As he stands by the counter, Aidan shows both surprise and relief on his face. Beside him is Liz, gentle and welcoming.

"It's wonderful to see you Jane," he tells her while introducing Liz to her as Nichole's aunt. He follows their initial polite exchanges by announcing "The Christmas cookie class starts tonight. I'd love it if you joined me."

My heart flutters. "I'd love to," I manage.

Holiday energy fills the bakery's back room that evening. Colorful sugar bowls and sprinkles sit beside rolling pins that make the stations shine. A chalkboard reads: Christmas Cookies deliver magic through each dash and create joy with every pinch. The instructor stands before us flour-dusted and bright-eyed as she claps her hands together. "Welcome, bakers! We will cream the butter and sugar until they reach the delicate texture of snow that has just fallen.

I take my place next to Aidan at our extended wooden counter. We both fasten our aprons and simultaneously measure the ingredients. I drop sugar into the bowl while he adds butter using a spoon. My hand brushes against Aidan's and everything else in the room disappears briefly.

With his voice barely audible he says, "Now add a touch of magic," while he folds flour into the mixture. I respond by playfully flicking a sprinkle of flour onto his cheek. His laughter fills the air with the comforting feeling of being home.

The instructor drifts between tables, offering tips. "Use a light hand—let the ingredients sing. The cookie-making experience transcends food as couples share giggles over sprinkles while friends compete to craft unique shapes and flour bursts into the air during festive fun.

I hold up my lopsided reindeer cookie. "What do you think?"

Aidan studies it, eyes soft. "It's perfect—full of character."

Our corner grows quiet as we place the last batch into the oven. Pride and warmth perform an intricate dance across Aidan's eyes as I look at him. I whisper "thank you" while my voice carries a hopeful weight. "This has been wonderful."

The timer's cheerful ding breaks our moment as he leans in closer. We both laugh, gathering the cooling cookies. The joyful sounds and delightful scents around me remind me that despite my dark history I can start anew right now.

Chapter 10

Nightmares

Jane's pov (Maria):

During quiet nights when daylight dims into darkness I remain awake with thoughts racing through my mind. My days bring endless joy as laughter fills the air and love surrounds me but when night falls I face terrifying flashes of fear and confusion once I close my eyes.

I experience pieces of a distant personal past which remains elusive in my memory but relentlessly fills me with intense emotions. My mind's eye shows me my younger self being swept away by reckless love during a whirlwind romance. The memory of an old boyfriend surfaces in my mind reminding me of how I once loved him before I treated him very badly. The memories jumble together: my nights of reckless fun in packed bars and the careless laughter that ended in a painful breakup which shattered my soul The image of his face flashes through my thoughts bringing back memories of unresolved emotional scars. Inwardly I scream, "Say my name! Who am I? Who was I?"

The nightmares drag me into debauched scenes of wild bar parties where my friends celebrated their privilege and excess. Their contemptuous stares hit me while their thoughtless comments echo around me making my shame weigh more than any regret. The chaos around me reveals only the smallest trace of my former self who existed before I chose isolation. My mind intentionally obscures times of happiness while expanding the cruelty I caused others and maybe to myself.

As I try to recall my parents' smiles and their loving gazes my mind reveals only the version of myself shaped by errors and wild behavior. I whisper to myself: Is that all there was to me? This realization causes my body to shake with deep shame and profound sorrow.

The darkness surrounds me while tears etch silent trails down my face and I start speaking a desperate monologue. With my voice reduced to a whisper I plead to God for assistance to mend the chasm in my thoughts. I promise to improve myself and stop the past from controlling my future. I strive to establish harmony between my past self and my developing identity, which now finds its meaning through nurturing love and familial bonds instead of temporary errors.

Through my haunted dreams I hunt for a spark of hope which tells me that these broken memories don't represent everything about my soul. Through patience and belief I understand that every broken fragment has the ability to heal itself with time and compassion. Throughout my struggle with fear I remain steadfast in believing my identity surpasses these dark visions. My journey includes developing trust alongside love and healing.

As darkness deepens around me I offer silent prayers while promising to seek out the positive things hidden beneath the confusion when tomorrow comes. Despite nightmares trying to engulf me, I maintain faith that my future will shine with light and redemption because of my present warmth and unwavering support from loved ones who help me become my true self.

Chapter 11

Tamales & Love

Jane's pov (Maria):

A full week has gone by with no updates on the missing persons investigation while Aidan and police teams continue searching the highway as if my car had disappeared without a trace. And the part for my phone? The phone part remains pending while a guarantee from China works through the delivery process. Yet these worries fade beside what awaits me today: I face a day richly filled with family bonds and cherished traditions while honoring tender love memories.

Before dawn breaks I open my eyes to the room's invasion by winter's pale gray light. I experience flashes from my mind's eye about a majestic house illuminated by Christmas lights while its halls shimmer with glitter and an unspoken sense of solitude fills the spaces. I remember wandering those halls as a child at Christmas: The surroundings were beautiful yet every decoration failed to eliminate the persistent cold. During those years Christmas appeared beautiful but remained distant as an event which never managed to touch my heart. Today might be the only day I will open my heart to experience the magic of Christmas and Aidan.

We hold our annual tamale-making celebration in the Martinez household with special enthusiasm. The house bursts with life: Every room buzzes with the joyful noise of relatives, neighbors, and beloved friends chatting and laughing together. A mix of simmering spice aromas and freshly ground masa fill the air as kitchen utensils clatter and friendly voices resonate from the busy kitchen space. The crowd flows around Liz whose gentle smile and warm presence brings a comforting glow to the festivities.

We assemble in the living room to witness a special unveiling before we start cooking. Jose the Reindeer rests on a small table that has been lovingly prepared while its fur shows signs of careful restoration and its eyes display a hopeful shine. The reindeer stands as the final present from Emma who was both Aidan's wife and Nichole's mother before she passed away. Through careful restoration this broken and forgotten object now embodies her gentle love and cherished beliefs within each stitch. The moment little Nichole steps into the room her eyes expand in amazement. Her trembling hands reach out to Jose as she longs to feel her mother's warmth through the touch.

"Jose is fixed!" she cries out while tears form at her eyes' edges. The room grows silent as all hearts stop before the sight of this humble restored reindeer which bears the weight of profound love and loss.

Aidan moves toward the center while speaking with a gentle and respectful tone. Emma desired for Nichole to keep a part of her with her as a symbol that love lasts.

We soon make our way to the celebration's heart: the kitchen. The long wooden tables display bowls filled with masa next to vibrant spices and meticulously arranged corn husks. Clad in a flour-dusted apron that makes her glow, my mother brings us all into her embrace.

With heartfelt dedication we craft each tamale which embodies our family's stories and traditions she declares her voice carrying the comforting warmth of morning sunlight.

I stand at the counter with determination but clumsiness in my movements. My fingers which lack experience in this tradition apply too much masa to each husk. Mama laughs softly while she tenderly touches my wrist to teach me how to make tamales with practiced movements and whispered teachings. My cousins and aunts work together in harmony while their shared laughter blends with the husks' gentle noise and the consistent tap of masa. Sarah and Liz share knowing smiles while adeptly shaping their tamales while Uncle Miguel adds playful teasing to the group which creates a relaxed atmosphere.

The kitchen buzzes with a joyful symphony: The kitchen fills with the sound of spices sizzling in pots while wooden spoons clatter together and old Christmas memories softly blend into conversation. Two cousins compete to create the best wrapped tamale while their playful rivalry brings joy to everyone present. Aidan playfully approaches the tamale meat to sneak a taste but receives a teasing scolding from my mother. She scolds Aidan for eating too much with "Save some for the rest of us!" while his playful smile causes my heart to beat faster.

The act of working allows me to experience how tradition reshapes my disjointed memories into meaningful moments of belonging. The joint effort of crafting something with love transforms my previous moments of solitude into shared experiences of connection. Each cheerful laugh and supportive word functions like a stitch that repairs the torn sections of my heart.

Nighttime arrives bringing the kitchen's reward of neatly packaged tamales with steam rising like murmured secrets. A palpable warmth from family gatherings fills the home together with a gentle sound of happiness. The living room becomes our gathering space as games like Charades and Pictionary generate laughter and intimate looks while each shared meal represents hope for a better future.

Once the celebration begins to fade, Aidan carefully transports sleeping Nichole to the truck. I step out into the chilly night where the cool air surrounds me and feels like winter giving me a gentle hug. The Christmas lights emit a soft glow that dances in Aidan's eyes while we remain together caught between the past day's memories and the quiet possibility of future moments. Slowly, he leans in. Our kiss begins tentatively yet promises to heal while expressing the freedom of letting go and a gentle love strong enough to fix what's been broken.

The moment he starts to say "I—" a distant chime from his truck softly cuts through the air. I smile while softly saying "It was perfect" as I try to hold onto the magic of the day through that brief kiss.

Eventually I find myself going back to my solitary space. The laughter sounds and tamales smell remain as a blessing that fills the air. The quiet space allows me to understand that today filled my emptiness with its messy yet beautiful traditions alongside the bittersweet gift of remembrance. I find myself learning to let my heart embrace the magic of Christmas and Aidan's love as I move from my past lonely celebrations to the warmth of family connections. My recollections stay blurred and disconnected yet tonight I permit myself to hope that this time I might truly be coming home.

Chapter 12

Phone Fixed

Jane's pov (Maria):

U pon entering the diner the following day I feel as though the entire world pauses in suspense. The familiar sound of clattering dishes and murmured conversation envelops me but my heart skips a beat when Sarah's cousin moves into the opposite booth. He lays my phone on the table. He whispers carefully while looking around with alert eyes, "The problem is now fixed." Picking up the phone makes my hands shake because its cold screen reveals memories from a buried past.

"Jane the device is completely charged and operational," he whispers.

I wrap my fingers around the device. I beg him with a whisper barely audible to keep this a secret.

He hesitates, then nods. "I promise."

I leave the diner while my heart races and my thoughts are overwhelmed by memories and uncertainty. What if I really was a monster? A criminal? The guilt I buried with my secrets is clawing its way back to the surface. I need time—time to face this alone.

I create a stomachache story to avoid eating dinner with Aidan's parents that night. I escape to my room and place the phone on my bed as if it were a silent oracle revealing my concealed secrets. My chest feels constricted while I look at my phone with my fingers resting above the lock screen. I take a shaky breath before tapping the screen.

Images and messages and emails bombard me in a sudden onslaught. My scrolling reveals past conversations that show my selfishness and immaturity in addition to my role in leading a movement to close the town's card factory which brought profit yet belonged to my family. The person I see in the photos seems unfamiliar to me because layers of time have obscured my memory of her.

I press myself to examine each condemning piece of information through my tear-smudged vision. The night stretches on, heavy with remorse. I pour cold water over my face wishing it could erase my past before realizing my reflection still bears a haunted appearance. As my chest pain intensifies I put on my coat and leave to search for Aidan.

The gentle snowfall blends with the twinkling Christmas lights while I walk. His hand connects with mine and his thumb moves in a soothing pattern along my knuckles. I hold onto that comforting warmth for a brief moment as I try to erase the phone's disclosures and my past life's shadows from my mind.

He guides me into a modest barn illuminated by fairy lights and fragrant with fresh flowers displayed on an unadorned table. His guitar rests against the wall. He clears his throat before showing me complete sincerity with his gaze. Jane, even though we've known each other for such a short time you need to know I'm falling very deeply for you. I... I wanted to show you something."

He starts with some hesitant strumming before he sings a hopeful, promising ballad. His voice trembles, each note a confession. The intensity of my chest constrictions causes tears to race down my cheeks. He offers his heart completely open to me while remaining ignorant of the "monster" that I believe myself to be. I am overcome with emotion so I cover my face with my hand before running into the night but leaving him alone to hear his song and my regret.

Inside my room I sob as the burden of my hidden truths crushes my spirit. The sound of a soft knock on the door causes me to jump. It's Grandma. I open the door for her and she immediately sits next to me without saying anything. Unable to contain myself I tell her everything from the phone to the messages to the choices that fill me with shame. Her eyes convey sorrow and steady love as she listens.

"Mija," she says softly while holding my shaking hand, "who are you now regardless of your past?"

I can't find an answer. My voice trembles and breaks into a fragile whisper when I say: "I... I don't know."

Her own eyes fill with tears. You're the girl who made tamales for us and comforted Nichole through her pain while working tirelessly during tough times. The person who helped me make tamales and comforted Nichole represents who you truly are instead of those errors on your phone.

I bury my face against her shoulder as my cries intensify. I am at a loss to understand how I can trust myself anymore.

She strokes my hair. "Then believe that God is leading you. The most challenging paths often lead to the most beautiful destinations.

I remain on the couch with Sarah and her parents feeling heavy and unsure as morning begins while gripping the phone. Every heartbeat pounds in my chest as I enter my mother's number into the phone.

"Hello? Mija?"

There's a tense breath from her that combines both relief and fear. "Hi, Mom."

"Oh, thank God! Where are you? What happened?"

My eyes burn with tears while I try to reconstruct my fragmented story which includes my amnesia and the Martinez family and tamale day. My speech emerges in uneven spurts that overflow with emotion.

Her whisper "Maria" triggers a rush of longing and pain within me.

"We thought we lost you," she whispers. My father and your mother prayed daily for your return to safety.

Their love consumes me while I feel the deep pain of finally belonging. My focus falters as I work to understand how the past version of me connects with the woman I am developing into.

"Mom… I'm sorry, I don't understand. I'm so lost…"

My father speaks through her voice crackling as his words carry both sadness and happiness. You've returned to us Maria our beloved child. We thought we'd lost you forever."

My shaking hand releases the phone while a wave of love and forgiveness engulfs me. Between us stand tearful apologies and heartfelt promises. That precise moment merges my fragmented history with the undeniable fact that we have reunited despite all obstacles.

Ending the phone call made me understand that my fragmented, ambiguous journey finally seems to guide me toward my true home.

Chapter 13

The Weight of Goodbye

Aidan's pov:

Aidan's Perspective:

The house is quieter than usual tonight. The remnants of holiday excitement persist but an intense silent heaviness permeates the atmosphere. From my truck outside my house I watch as frost forms intricate designs across the windshield. The steering wheel presses so forcefully against my palms that waves of tension move through my arms but I cannot bring myself to turn the ignition.

Maria who I call my Maria but others know as Jane is about to leave. Maria gathers her limited belongings inside while getting ready to return to an unfamiliar world that excludes both of us. A wounding idea spirals through my chest like a sharp blade.

I yearn to enter the house and call out words that could persuade her to stay but my vocabulary fails me. I seek refuge in my work because it is where I excel. I head toward the barn which acts as a sanctuary for genuine work and uncomplicated responsibilities. Yet even as I lose myself in the repetitive motions of fixing, cleaning, and mending, every detail around me reminds me of her: Her nose scrunches up with focus when she folds napkins at the diner while her determined expression shows when she works with tamale dough despite her charming clumsiness and her laughter rings clear as she sleds with Nichole. The look she gave me before she started running showed her eyes full of both hope and longing.

My mind constantly revisits our shared moments while being tormented by the admission I now wish I had kept silent. It was a mistake to reveal my feelings to her so early on. I should have waited.

As Christmas Eve unfolds I depart from my home to reach the cemetery which stands serene beneath a soft snowfall. My feet move towards Emma's headstone without my awareness as loss and yearning direct my steps. I kneel on the untouched snow as I gently erase the fragile frost covering her name.

I mutter to the empty air about my repeated failures while feeling regret and longing for redemption from a man who knows he has lost direction. I slowly bend forward to place a fresh bouquet at her grave while each petal serves as a delicate memorial for love that remains strong through the years.

I release another trembling sigh and speak as though Emma might still listen to my words. Back then I believed Jose the Reindeer was nothing but a meaningless toy. The toy never held just one meaning for me. That toy is our memory, our anchor. Each picture and every laugh or tear holds a permanent fragment of you and us together. You'll always remain with us Emma regardless of what life brings.

I gently press my hand against the cold stone while trying to absorb her silent strength. I admit softly and with hesitation that I have found someone special at last. "Her name is Maria. My biggest worry is that I might have frightened her away from our relationship. Matters of the heart have always been challenging for me. I long to trust in her and our relationship but fear that I'll make the same errors again.

My spoken words drift away with the wind into the silent space. "Emma, I could really use your advice. How do I fix this? What steps should I take to ensure Maria stays with me even though I have doubts and hesitations?

The memory of Emma combined with Jose the Reindeer's role as her spirit's keeper for Nichole and everyone else anchors me in that quiet sacred space. It is a bittersweet reminder that even in our deepest losses, something binds us together: The bond that keeps us connected in the midst of profound losses stems from love combined with memory and the persistent hope we hold for redemption.

I shut my eyes while yearning for guidance from bygone days to help me gather the courage to connect with Maria before time runs out.

Maria's Perspective:

My parents reach our house on Christmas Eve morning. When I open the door, they stand there— my mother on one side, my father on the other— and for a moment I see strangers: These faces that I know well have become strangers because they do not match my heart anymore. Their features soften with relief though their eyes still show tension that silently questions if I remain part of their world.

The truth is my biological family exists and I recognize them but their presence does not bring me the same comforting feeling as I experience with the Martinez family. My mother, in a gentle gesture I've witnessed a thousand times, brushes a stray curl from my face and softly asks, "Mija, are you ready?" That simple act unleashes a flood of recollections: The sound of a passing train joins the memories of my isolated youth with my father's tender chuckles and my mother's loving chastisements in quick Spanish when I acted out. My life with Aidan and Nichole comes back to me in clear snapshots of his unwavering support and her infectious enthusiasm along with shared moments of joy from making tamales and sled rides through snowy landscapes.

63

The memories crash over me. I gasp and hold my head tightly when emotions surge through me.

"I am Maria Victoria Consuela Cruz. My family originated in Argentina but we currently reside in a New York City penthouse.

I turn to my father and my voice quivers as I say "Papá…" with tears in my eyes.

His arms encircle me without delay. I cry into his shoulder, "I remember. I remember everything."

My mother holds my hand tightly while tears stream down her face as she whispers "Gracias a Dios." A mix of relief and sorrow emerges but is quickly followed by a chilling dread. With every heartbeat I become aware of my true identity but hold fear that Aidan will never extend forgiveness.

The chaotic scene around me becomes the backdrop for my final tearful farewell with Aidan's family. I move step by step into the dimly lit entrance hall. Aidan's parents wrap me up in a gentle hug as his mother speaks softly with tears in her eyes advising me to follow God's path, "mija." His father takes my hand and communicates unwavering support through his silent promise of acceptance. Little Nichole tugs my sleeve as she pleads with her tiny voice saying "Don't go" while Sarah holds my other hand. I want you to stay."

Nichole places the lovingly restored Jose the Reindeer gently onto my unsteady hands. Her pleading eyes filled with hope and tears shine as she begs, "Please remember us." I grasp the reindeer tightly and sense all its repaired stitches while remembering Emma's love and realizing that my past has to intersect with my present for me to decide my future. My deepest fear lies in the possibility that my departure will mean I am leaving behind the person I never wished to lose.

As they bid me goodbye the warmth of their words and touches envelop me like a delicate cocoon, making each moment etch itself into my heart. Every tear and gentle smile shows a fresh start as I carry both my past burdens and future hopes.

Finally, my father's voice breaks the spell. I walk behind him to the waiting limo without feeling because my eyes remain locked on the reindeer I hold and the faces I leave behind. Nichole's soft plea reverberates in my thoughts—"So you won't forget us"—while a tear escapes my eye as the limo drives off toward a future that feels both known and painfully strange.

Chapter 14

The Chase

Aidan's pov:

I'm standing in the cemetery, fresh snow like a silent shroud over every gravestone, and I'm drowning in regret and longing. The hush presses down on me as I replay every choice, every moment of weakness that brought me back here. "I don't know what to do," I murmur into the still air. "I thought I could let her go... that it'd be easier if I stopped chasing what I can't have." A cold wind sighs through the barren trees, offering nothing but the raw ache of my unresolved heartache.

Then a sharp voice cuts through the quiet. "Then what the hell are you doing here?" I spin around. Sarah stands a few feet behind me, bundled in her coat, arms crossed, concern and exasperation etched on her face.

"You're at a grave when you should be at an airport," she snaps, urgency and care tangled in her tone.

Words clamber up my throat, but she barges on. "Just what? Sitting here, wallowing in regret, convincing yourself it's too late?" She steps closer, gaze fixed on me. "You love her, Aidan. Don't talk to Emma about it—go tell Maria before it's too late."

A jolt of clarity surges through me. I clench my fists, steadying myself. "I know," I whisper. In that instant, I decide: I'm going after her.

Sarah's expression softens into a relieved smile. "Took you long enough," she teases, grabbing my arm and dragging me toward her truck. "Come on. We're leaving."

The tires spin up slush as I gun the engine, my knuckles white on the wheel. My heart hammers faster than ever—faster than when I lost Maria the first time, faster than when I told myself I'd never love again. She's at the airport, almost gone, and I refuse to let it happen.

Sarah's phone buzzes with frantic messages. "Hurry!" she urges. In the backseat, little Nichole bounces anxiously. "You're gonna stop her, right, Daddy? You have to stop her!" she pleads, voice small and urgent.

"I will," I promise more to myself than to them. I slam my foot on the gas. The engine roars, an old country love song drifts from the radio, but it fades as each second stretches into eternity.

When the airport finally comes into view, time slows. I skid into the lot, feeling every moment in slow motion: passengers hustling, footsteps echoing, snow glinting under the lights. I kill the engine and leap out, sprinting toward the entrance with Sarah and Nichole racing behind me.

Inside, farewells swirl all around—hugs, tears, hasty goodbyes. My breath is ragged as I scan the crowd until I see her at the security checkpoint. Maria stands framed by her parents, pride and tension in their faces. In her arms she clutches Jose the Reindeer, that ragged but beloved symbol that's always bound us together.

"Maria!" I shout, desperation ripping through my voice.

Her head snaps around. Shock widens her eyes as I push through the crowd. My heart pounds so hard I'm sure it'll burst. "Wait! Don't go," I cry, voice carrying over the din.

She hesitates, lips parting. "Aidan—" she begins, but I cut her off. Words tumble out, raw and urgent: "I love you. I should've told you sooner. I should've fought for you sooner." Each syllable is weighted with regret and longing, hanging between us in the charged air.

Tears well in her eyes. "Aidan—" she whispers, torn between fear and hope.

I take a step closer, my voice softening. "I don't care about your past, Maria. I don't care who you were. I care about who you are now—the woman who makes the goofiest tamales, even when they

68

flop, the woman who patched up Jose for a little girl who needed him, the woman who made me feel alive again. Please don't leave. Stay with me. Stay with Nichole, with us."

In that breathless moment, Nichole dashes forward and clings to Maria's waist, burying her face in her coat. "Please don't go! We love you!" she sobs.

Maria stands frozen, clutching that ragged reindeer. Then, with a shuddering exhale, she drops her boarding pass. She turns to me and wraps her arms around me. "I love you, Aidan," she whispers, voice thick with emotion. "Mom, can we spend Christmas here?"

Behind us Sarah laughs through relieved tears. "Thank God," she murmurs. I hug Maria tighter, my heart swelling with hope. "You're home, Maria. You've always been home."

Our eyes meet amid the terminal chaos, and I lean in to kiss her—a kiss that speaks of redemption, second chances, and the Christmas magic that brought us back together.

Epilogue

Three Years Later

Maria's pov:

My living room offers a warm ambiance as fresh pine and cinnamon aromas permeate the space while the Christmas tree emits a gentle sparkle. Stockings hang above the fireplace—each one embroidered with a name: The stockings above the fireplace now include one for little Mateo along with Aidan's, mine, and Nichole's. I watch as laughter bubbles up around me: The floor becomes a playful battleground for Nichole and Mateo among scattered wrapping paper and family revelry while Aidan rests on the couch close to me with one arm around my shoulders and his hand touching my leg. Living this life alongside this love in the home we built together feels surreal.

I draw closer to Aidan's warmth while whispering my disbelief at his airport drive that day.

Tears well up in my eyes as I observe Nichole's radiant smile directed at her baby brother who holds Jose the Reindeer, our precious symbol of true significance. Her innocent happiness brings me a smile because all past memories and difficulties have intensified this joy.

I need to tell you that Christmas captured my heart when I shared my story. I fell for Aidan. I maintain my faith that God provides solutions through His infinite wisdom for every situation. My transition from darkness to this season's light meant rediscovering Christmas magic and discovering true love and a family that felt like home.

With my heart wide open I live each day appreciating the miracles that occur when you trust both love and God's guiding hand. The story I live is ongoing because it celebrates my constructed life and holds the promise that all endings lead to new beginnings.

Acknowledgments

First and foremost, I thank God for blessing me with another day of life and the opportunity to share this story with you.
A heartfelt thank you to Melisa Olivarez for your unwavering support—it truly means the world to me.
To my mom and dad, and to all my familia, I love you all more than words can express! This journey took me years to bring to life, and I hope I make you all proud.

Ernest Olivarez was born and raised in Saginaw, Michigan. He is married to Melisa Olivarez and is a proud father of five children—Michael, Isaiah, Luke, Arron, and Nichole—while cherishing the memory of Alexis, his angel in Heaven.

He is also a loving grandfather to Delilah, Isabella, and Alinah. By profession, Ernest works as an electrical engineer, but his true passion lies in storytelling. In his free time, he enjoys spending time with his family, writing and producing stories and music, and volunteering at his church.

To learn more about him and his work, visit Ernest.Olivarez.com.

Other books by Ernest Olivarez

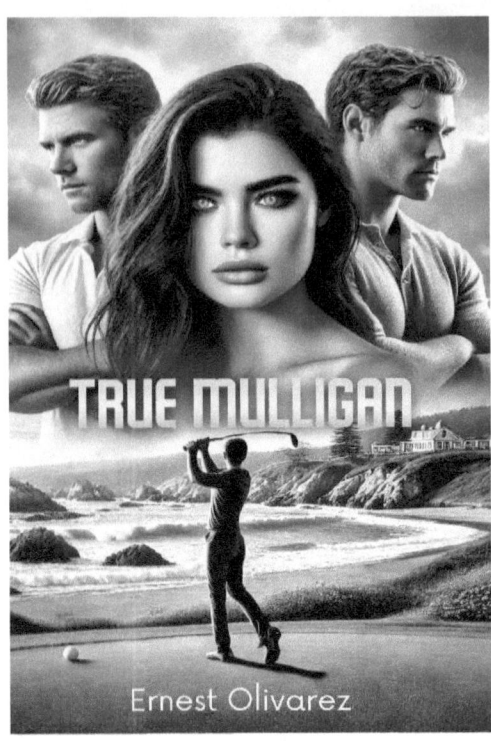

A fallen golf prodigy fights for redemption at the U.S. Open, battling the rival who once was his closest friend, the ghosts of his past, and the love he's on the verge of losing—only to discover that his greatest victory won't be found on the course.

True Mulligan is a gripping sports drama about redemption, rivalry, and discovering that some wins are worth more than trophies.

A lost map. A forgotten legend. A secret that could change everything.

When Nate Allen and his friends, Jenny and Jackson, pull a drowning kid from the raging river, they think their adventure is over. But hidden inside an old Bible, they uncover a map that whispers of something bigger—something tied to an outlaw's last great secret.

At first, it's just a game. A way to shake up their boring Texas town. But as they follow the clues, they realize they aren't the only ones searching. Someone else is watching. Someone who will stop at nothing to keep the past buried.

Now, it's not just about treasure—it's about survival.

A high-stakes mystery packed with history, action, and danger! Perfect for fans of Spy School and National Treasure!

José the Reindeer is an award-winning bilingual book that celebrates Latino heritage and tells the heartwarming story of how someone a little different saves Christmas when Santa gets stuck in San Antonio. When you purchase the complete box set, you become part of the José family! Be ready—your plush José toy comes with a unique certificate of adoption, where he officially takes on your family's last name.

José becomes a cherished part of your family gatherings and holiday traditions. Your kids can hold him, love him, move him around, and take pictures— there are no complicated rules to follow! He is now part of your loving home and will follow your traditions.

The adoption certificate also includes a special pledge to share love, joy, and peace during Christmas. We can't wait to see how your family welcomes José! Be sure to share your special moments with him on social media—we'd love to see your holiday traditions come to life!

https://www.josethereindeer.com/

www.ingramcontent.com/pod-product-compliance
Lightning Source LLC
Chambersburg PA
CBHW031859170626
46807CB00004B/1807